For Am...

Badger
the
Mystical Mutt

and the Flying Fez

Lyn McNicol

McNicol & Jackson

THE LUNICORN PRESS

THE LUNICORN PRESS
Glasgow
Text © Lyn McNicol and Laura Cameron Jackson 2014
Illustrations © Laura Cameron Jackson 2014
All rights reserved

First published 2014 by The Lunicorn Press

1

Printed by Martins the Printers, Berwick-upon-Tweed
Designed and typeset by Heather MacPherson at Raspberry
Creative Type
Set in 14.25 pt Gentium Book

British Library Cataloguing in Publication Data
A CIP catalogue record for this book is available from the British
Library

ISBN: 978-0-9569640-6-9

www.badgerthemysticalmutt.com
www.facebook.com/badgermutt
www.twitter.com/badgermutt

*For Brian and Janet McNicol & Olive
and Gordon Henry*

A round of "up-paws" for *Badger the Mystical Mutt*

"*A fun, fast-paced romp of a read for younger readers ... terrific stuff!*"
Cathy Cassidy

"*Pitch-perfect subtlety and wit.*"
Shari Low

"*Badger the Mystical Mutt has quickly become a firm favourite with children beginning to read on their own.*"
Off the Page, Stirling Book Festival

"*Badger does help bring a smile to your face with his unusual approach to magic making.*"
Missing Sleep

"*There are some underlying morality themes that should allow vigorous class discussions.*"
Stephen King, The School Librarian Magazine

"*Once again McNicol & Jackson have come up with a brilliant story where Badger and his mystical powers are called upon to help out his friends.*"
BFK Books

"*Kids' book takes world by storm.*"
The Scottish Sun

ALSO BY MCNICOL & JACKSON

Badger the Mystical Mutt

Badger the Mystical Mutt and the
Barking Boogie

Badger the Mystical Mutt and the
Crumpled Capers

Badger the Mystical Mutt and the
Daydream Drivers

Badger the Mystical Mutt and the
Enchanting Exchange

E-books from The Badger the
Mystical Mutt series are also available via
the usual outlets

Chapter One

It was Old Year's Night and just a whisker away from an epic pea-souper.

Badger the Mystical Mutt was getting ready for the party of all parties, the grooviest of get-togethers and the swankiest of shindigs ever to happen on the lane: a gang reunion. Pickle, the one remaining member of the gang, had seen her best friend, Pogo Paws leave to rejoin his childhood circus, and she was still feeling miffed. To cheer her up, Badger had decided to throw a party in the lane for some of her old friends.

Badger stretched to hang some more red and white polka-dotted bunting on the washing line of his garden, except that he couldn't see the rope for the fog.

This is the foggiest fog I've ever seen. I hope everyone will be able to get here without any problems, he thought to himself.

Just then, he heard a kerfuffle at the bottom of the garden.

"Oh Badger, can't you do anything to get rid of this fog?" shouted Pickle, tumbling through the crack in the fence. "Where are you anyway?"

"Over here!" yelled Badger, as he watched his fed-up friend clamber towards him.

"It's terrific that you're organising this party Badger, but it just won't be the same without Pogo Paws," grumbled Pickle.

"I know, Pickle, but it will still be amazing to see Top Dog, Dodgy Dave, Snif and Lennie again."

"I suppose so." She sighed and looked at the Mystical Mutt with a puzzled expression. "Is that your new look, Badger?"

"What do you mean, Pickle?"

"Where's your neckerchief?" She pointed.

Badger's paws sped to his neck in horror. His neck was completely bare. It was true! His beloved 'Chief wasn't there. His eyes darted around in a panic.

"I don't know! I had it on as usual this morning. I never took it off, and I never noticed it unravelling. Maybe it came off when I was collecting the bunting."

Badger and Pickle bumbled about in the dense mist searching the garden for the lost neckerchief.

"Maybe it's just gone to get spruced up for the party," said Badger hopefully. "Although 'Chief usually tells me when it disappears for a wash." He frowned.

"Uh oh! This is serious, Badger," grimaced Pickle "How can you do your magic without 'Chief?"

Badger gulped. "I know, Pickle, this is possibly the worst thing that's ever happened to me. We have to find it before the others start to arrive."

He fell silent. Pickle shifted uneasily from paw to paw.

"Right," said Badger, "I'll do my Search and Find spell, and hope that works. He took a deep breath and uttered the magic words: *Jeepers creepers, finders keepers, let 'Chief appear before my peepers!"*

He stood back and crossed his paws ... but nothing happened.

"We can't see *anything* in this fog, Badger, with or without your dodgy spells," moaned Pickle.

"Well, do you have a better idea?" fretted Badger.

"I know you're upset, but we'll find it," said Pickle, "Why don't you keep checking your garden. and I'll go and have a sniff up the lane?"

Badger nodded sadly and waved Pickle away.

As Pickle crept through the creeping fog in search of 'Chief, Badger fumbled in the gloom, muttering his *Finders Keepers* spell over and over again, and talking to himself."This is a nightmare! Without 'Chief, my badgical magicalness will never be as badgical magical. What am I going to do?"

Just then, a very glum Pickle returned.

"I tried, Badger. I really tried. I've sniffed the length and breadth of the lane, but I can't find any trace of 'Chief."

Badger sighed heavily.

"That's me scuppered, Pickle. Now it's definitely *Losers Weepers*," whimpered the Mystical Mutt.

"What are you going to do?" she asked.

"I don't know!" howled Badger.

"What will help you on your magical missions?"

"I don't know!" he bawled.

"What will help you fly, protect you, and make you look like the dandiest dog on the lane?"

"I don't know, I don't know, I don't know!" shouted Badger, hanging his head.

"Right, Badger, pull yourself together! This is just a blip, and not helped by the fact that we can't see a thing in this fog," said Pickle, taking charge. "There's a big party happening tonight, with nearly all of our friends. Surely, there must be someone who can help?"

"There isn't!" moaned Badger wearily, sitting down on the damp grass. Suddenly, he sprang upwards and yelled: "Oh — yes — there — is!"

His eyebrows twitched and his eyes brightened as he remembered his old friend.

"Otto!" he hollered.

"Who on earth is Otto?" asked Pickle.

"Otto is my back-up and my substitute for when 'Chief goes for his yearly wash. He's a flying fez!"

"A flying what?" she gasped.

"A flying *fez*, with a tickly tassle. I'm sure he's around here somewhere, if I can just remember the spell. Now let me think ..."

Sparkles of light appeared around Badger as he rummaged gleefully in his plant plot. He patted his head.

"Bring me sunshine, just like that,
With a little bit of this, and a little bit of that,
With a ring-a-ding-ding and a rat-a-tat-tat,
Now show me Otto: the bright red hat!"

Badger stood back and waited. His plant pot began to tremble and rumble noisily.

Starbursts of light erupted from the pot and sped into the sky, twinkling brightly in the fog.

All at once, something burst from the depths of the pot and knocked Badger off balance. It swooshed and whizzed around the garden, giggling wildly. Badger and Pickle ducked and dived below the perky U(nidentified) F(lying) O(bject).

"Is that thing Otto?" shrieked Pickle, as she fell to the ground to avoid the low-flying fez.

"I sincerely hope so!" shouted Badger, joining her on the grass.

Badger wondered if he'd got the spell right, or if he'd conjured up a troublesome sprite instead. On top of everything else, that was all he needed!

Chapter Two

"Hah, gotcha!" squealed a voice as something landed on top of Badger's head. "It's about time you called upon my services. But you'll have to catch me first!"

Otto the Fez swirled around Badger, tickling him with his black feathery tassle, until he fell onto the grass laughing.

Pickle looked on, speechless.

"Who's your friend then?" asked Otto cheekily.

"This, my dear Otto, is Pickle. She's been helping me try to find 'Chief.'"

"Pickle? Tickle Pickle. Pickly Tickly," said Otto, zooming towards her.

"Uh oh!" said Pickle, running into the shed for shelter.

"Come here at once!" ordered Badger.

The fez fluttered around the Mystical Mutt's head and declared: "Make me ..."

"Now, Otto, come on, I really need you to help me. It's Old Year's Night; a really special time when we say goodbye to the old and welcome in the new. And my neckerchief is missing. So can you just try to behave, please?"

"But I hardly ever get out to play nowadays. I haven't flown for ages. You only ever call on me when you want something," huffed Otto.

"Otto," said Badger calmly, "we've talked about this before. You know fine well that you are 'Chief's stand-in. *Of course*, I only call you when I want something. That's the whole point. Now, stop feeling so sorry for yourself. There will be plenty of time for flying later."

The fez hovered silently in the mist for a moment, then shot sharply upwards. He swooped down, barrel-rolled between the bunting, looped around the washing line and landed with a cheeky flick of his tassle at Badger's feet.

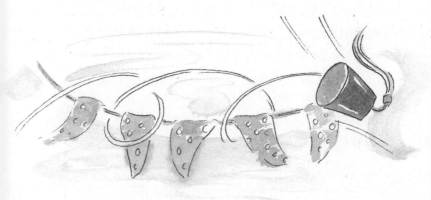

Badger rolled his eyes.

"Why can't I fly now?" asked Otto petulantly.

"It looks like you just have. Surely you can see how low the visibility is. It's dangerous. This has to be a no-fly zone until the fog clears. I'm only thinking of your safety after all," said Badger sensibly. "Now, come here and pay attention for once in your life, I need some help while 'Chief is absent."

The little fez glided on to Badger's head reluctantly.

"'Chief muttered something about going off on a top-secret mission, and that you'd probably need my help," said Otto. "But nobody said I had to behave."

"'Chief told *you*?" shouted Badger in disbelief.

"Of course! We magical mascots must stick together, after all," replied Otto haughtily.

"Even so, I'm surprised. 'Chief didn't mention it to me," said Badger, rubbing his neck.

"Oh, Badger," sighed Otto pompously, "there are some secrets that even you, the Mystical Mutt, simply cannot be trusted with."

Badger frowned. "Did 'Chief say when he's coming back?"

"Might have," said Otto

"So, when then?" asked Badger with increasing impatience.

"Not telling!" Otto giggled, shaking his tassle.

"Is that your final answer?" said Badger wearily.

"Absolutely! Yes!"

"So, I'm stuck with you?"

"It looks like it," sniggered Otto, tickling Badger's ears, "Now, let's have some fun."

"Tame that tickling tassle for tonight, *please*," begged Badger, wandering off to the bottom of his garden where he sniffed a freshly delivered p-mail.

"Excellent!" he said. "It's a note from my cousin, the Earl of Doodlepoppington. He's on his way. I hope he brings us a hamper of luxury goodies."

There was an almighty crash from the lane. Badger peered through the crack in the fence to see two shapes rumbling around with bin lids.

"You've arrived then?" smiled Badger.

Hamish and Top Dog stood up and shook themselves.

"I'm sure my ears are getting longer," said Hamish. "I couldn't see where I was going in this fog. Where's your neckerchief, Badger? Is it being washed?"

"Hello, my old friend. We've brought a feast of Crunchy Munchy Chewy Chops for the party, and most importantly, a higgledy-piggledy tower of toast, especially for you. You don't look quite yourself without that red spotty thing. Where is it?" added Top Dog.

"I'm afraid 'Chief has disappeared," said Badger, hugging them both warmly.

Top Dog and Hamish looked at each other in astonishment. They couldn't believe that the famous neckerchief was not where it should be; knotted around Badger's neck. Badger sighed sadly.

"I don't really know how I'm going to cope without 'Chief. But we have a party to organise, so I have to rely on Otto for just now."

"Who's Otto?" asked Top Dog.

Badger grinned nervously and pointed to the top of his head.

Top Dog and Hamish peered warily at the little red hat.

"Now," winked Badger, feeling his tummy rumble, "if you'll please excuse me for a moment, I have some urgent toast business to attend to." And he ran off to the shed to stash his toast.

Inside his shed, Badger spoke to Pickle, who was still in hiding from the pesky fez. "Your old pal Top Dog has arrived with Hamish. You need to go and mingle, and I need to pack away this toast."

Pickle joined the others and immediately spotted the Crunchy Munchy Chewy Chops.

Top Dog gave her a high paw and said, "Hello, Pickle. Are you still causing your usual chaos in the lane?"

"Well, I do try, since I'm the only *true* remaining member of the old gang. You know Pogo Paws left to join the circus, don't you?"

"Yes, I heard, but now you've got Badger as a pal."

"Maybe, but it's not the same," she sighed, edging closer to the bag of Crunchy Munchy Chewy Chops.

"Pickle, no! They're for the party. You have to wait till later," chided Hamish, pushing her paw away as she tried to snaffle them.

Just then, all heads pointed up the lane as they heard a distant tap and shuffle, and voices drawing closer. A *'cha cha cha'* sound swished through the fog, and a spotlight appeared, as a glitter ball hovered in the air.

Badger emerged from his shed.

"That can only be Dodgy Dave and Cheryl, home at last, from their sell-out dancing tour of Blackpool," chuckled Badger.

Top Dog, Hamish, Pickle and Badger watched as a vision of glamour emerged through the mist. Dodgy Dave and Cheryl danced towards them with disco lights flashing behind them.

Cheryl swirled and curtsied and Dodgy Dave uttered a gruff "hello".

"We have lights, do you have the camera? And is this where the action is?" sparkled Cheryl.

As they all huddled around hugging and high-pawing, Cheryl piped up: "Shine the spotlight over here, Dodgy Dave. I have to show everyone my boasting book."

"Your boasting book?" asked Pickle.

"Yes, it's just a small selection of newspaper clippings of us on tour. Obviously they focus mainly on me and my gorgeous ball gowns, but Dodgy Dave does get a mention as well."

Pickle groaned, Top Dog grinned and Badger beamed with pride.

"Awesome!" smiled Hamish.

Meanwhile, Otto had sneaked off Badger's head and flown towards the shed.

"I think this calls for some toast," said Badger kindly.

The Mystical Mutt disappeared into his shed, and returned moments later with a tower of higgledy-piggledy toast.

They chomped away hungrily, and quickly wolfed it down. One by one, noses twitched, whiskers wobbled and eyes watered, as the gang let out almighty sneezes and splutters.

"Yuk!" they yelled.

"That tastes awful!" cringed Pickle.

"It's certainly not your usual delicious slice," said Top Dog, scrunching his eyes.

"Your toast isn't the same. Your neckerchief isn't here. What's been happening whilst we've been away, Badger?" frowned Dodgy Dave. Badger shook his head and sneezed again.

"It's pepper!" he shouted. "My toast has been tampered with. Who would do such a thing?"

Badger looked towards the shed, where Otto was sniggering at the window.

"That wretched fez!" barked Badger. "I told him to behave! It's one thing to go around tickling, but *no one* messes with my toast!"

"I thought *that* thing was just Badger's party hat!" grunted Dodgy Dave, "but it looks like the same old *waggery* is still going on in the lane.

"But that hat doesn't even have a tail," laughed Top Dog.

"I'd quite like to try a tassle for a tail!" said Hamish.

Dodgy Dave and Top Dog shook their heads in bewilderment.

Whilst Badger went to sort Otto out, Pickle rubbed her eyes, pointed at Top Dog and Dodgy Dave and said: "That's how *we* used to be, getting up to high jinks and causing mischief. Look what's happened to you both: Dodgy Dave, you're the king of dance, and Top Dog, you're a *pet!* Don't you miss the old days? This is supposed to be a reunion, but it's not really, is it? You're different dogs."

Top Dog nodded wisely, as Dodgy Dave adjusted his star-spangled collar and shrugged.

"We *are* different dogs, Pickle, but for the better," said Top Dog. "Look at me now. I've got a home. I've got Big Folk to look after me, and a best pal in Hamish. I'm too tired to chase nonsense these days."

"You mean you're lazy!" scoffed Pickle.

Top Dog shrugged.

"Well, you can't say *I'm* lazy," snorted Dodgy Dave. "I work harder now than I ever did when I was on the street: touring every day, and dancing every night."

"I just wish the old gang could be truly back together as we were originally ... and that includes Pogo Paws," sighed Pickle.

As Badger returned with Otto, flashing lights pierced the fog in the lane. Then, they heard lots of huffing and puffing, clanking and clunking, followed immediately by an enormous *crash, bang* and *wallop*! They rushed to the end of the garden and looked out.

There was Badger's famous travelling machine, the Wim-Wim for a Wowser, wedged firmly between the fences.

"Oh no!" groaned Badger. "My garden solar lights can't be seen in this weather. The disco lights in the lane must look like a landing strip."

One by one they leapt through the crack in the fence to see the damage that had been done. But as smoke billowed out from below the Wim-Wim and steam hissed out from its sides, Badger knew it didn't look good. Apart from his poor injured Wim-Wim, if the lane was blocked, the party could not go ahead.

"Could this day get any worse?" he sighed as the Wim-Wim coughed out a splutter.

Chapter Three

"Dodgy Dave, shine those spotlights over here!" shouted Badger, nodding to where the Wim-Wim was stuck in the lane.

The dog pointed the powerful beams up the lane, but the fog was so dense that all that resulted was a ghostly glow.

"I need an illumination spell and then an unjamming spell. That's a *lot* to manage without my trusty 'Chief'" sighed Badger.

"Did someone mention jamming?" purred Velvet Viv, one of the local alley cats. She was joined by her pals, Trixie Rose and Silky Smith, who slunk along the lane, dragging a curious contraption behind them.

"We heard you were having a party, Badger, so we've brought the Meowzik Maker. We'll be your DJs for the evening," announced Trixie.

Badger raised his eyebrows. "Disc jockeys?"

"Oh, are horses coming to the party, too?" asked Hamish hopefully.

"DJs! Of course! I do love a dog in a dinner jacket," smiled Cheryl dreamily.

"Actually the D is for Diva, and the J is for Jivers," sighed Silky.

"Great," said Badger, "if this party *ever* gets started."

The cats' eyes widened and glittered with the excitement of being in charge of the tunes for the evening.

"Cats eyes!" Badger exclaimed. "That's it! Can they really light the way? Can you help me see what has caused the Wim-Wim to get stuck?"

"Our eyes are just another two of our many beautiful gifts. Follow me," purred Trixie, leading and lighting the way.

Badger crept behind Trixie, Silky and Velvet Viv towards where the Wim-Wim was wedged.

The cats' eyes lit up the travelling machine from below. Badger could see now what had happened. In the fog, the Wim-Wim had tried to land, and missing his garden, had plummeted into the narrow lane at an awkward angle. Its undercarriage was firmly jammed.

"Thanks, Cats. I can see now what needs to be done. Otto!" shouted Badger. summoning his fez.

The little red hat zoomed quickly to Badger's head.

"I have to remember the unjamming spell. Can you help me?" asked Badger hopefully.

"Of course, Badger. Just

tell me what I can do," said Otto, being unusually obedient.

"I need some butter, soap and hot water."

Otto sped off to the garden to fetch the required ingredients for the spell, whilst Badger scratched his head trying to remember the rhyme. As Otto returned with the various bits and bobs, Badger threw them all into his plant pot and began:

"Willow-stick and jewel bug scram,
Candlewick and chowder clam,
Knobs of butter and roasted yam,
Shimmy the soap and now ... UNJAM!"

Badger stood back feeling rather pleased with himself, but his smile soon turned to one of horror as he watched the lane fill with sticky strawberry jam and thousands of peas.

"Oh no! I must have got it wrong!" Badger frowned.

Otto raced gleefully towards the delicious mess and started scooping up hatfuls, because at exactly the same time as Badger had been performing his spell, Otto had hovered above, whispering a countercharm: *"With a block of cheese instead of butter, make jam and frozen peas go splutter."*

Badger looked at Otto suspiciously. He checked his ingredients in the plant pot, and discovered that the butter had been replaced with a block of mouldy cheddar. He threw it aside.

"Otto!" shouted Badger firmly, "Get back here now! You're supposed to be helping me, not making things worse!"

Otto flew to Badger's head and sat on top cautiously.

"It was only a joke! Don't take it so seriously," said the fez.

"'Chief would never overrule my spells, Otto. I'm really disappointed. Isn't there a mascot code of honour?"

"Yes, there is, but it only exists when we are valued and made to feel worthwhile." Otto fidgeted.

Badger shook his head in exasperation and sighed.

"Right, I'll try again."

"With soapy lathers and a bit of luck,
Please widen the fences and come unstuck
And while you're at it, clear this mess,
And make the party a great success."

All at once, the fences on either side of the Wim-Wim creaked and moved further apart. It shot immediately upwards into the thick sky. The jam vanished and the peas rolled away.

Dodgy Dave shone his spotlight towards Badger's garden. There, the alley cats lay on their backs to form a landing strip, their vivid eyes pointing towards the sky. Soon, the Wim-Wim came into view and made its descent to land safely in the garden.

Badger breathed a heavy sigh of relief, until he spotted Otto flapping his tassle around the top of the Wim-Wim.

"Otto!" shouted Badger sternly "Get down here now! I told you this was a no-fly zone."

The little fez returned and fanned his tassle over Badger's eyes. The Mystical Mutt stumbled blindly around the garden, wishing and hoping his beloved 'Chief would return as soon as possible.

As the alley cats set up their Meowzik Maker in the lane, Cheryl decorated the bins with fairy lights. Top Dog, Dodgy Dave and Pickle chatted more about their bygone antics as a gang.

Then out of the blue, Otto began to whizz around excitedly above them all. He pointed his tassle towards the crack in the fence. Everyone looked that way to see their old pals Snif and Timmy, the cat with the crumpled ear, arrive.

"Hello everyone. We come bearing magical mead, made with merriment and mirth," grinned Snif, full of cheer.

Badger, Top Dog, Dodgy Dave and Pickle rushed to welcome them back.

"It's great you could make it. I know how busy you are over at PLOPP, especially at this time of year," smiled Badger.

"PLOPP? Please tell me that's not a portable pooper scooper?" winced Dodgy Dave.

"Hah! No, my friend!" said Snif. "You left before we set it up. It's a drop-in centre for strays. It's called PLOPP for short: the *Peaceful Living Organisation for Pooches and Pussycats.* We provide food, bedding and a few home comforts until our clients are rehomed."

"You mean you work side by side with ... *the homeless?*" said Dodgy Dave scornfully.

Everyone fell silent until Velvet Viv piped up. "Oi, shut it, dancer boy! We all helped you win the *Barking Boogie,* remember, when you were a stray on the lane."

"It might be all high kicks and glamour for you now, Dodgy Dave, but you were once homeless too," scowled Pickle.

"Never forget where you've come from," added Top Dog.

Dodgy Dave hung his head in shame. "You're right. I'm sorry Snif and Timmy. It's truly admirable what you are doing. I wish PLOPP had existed when I was on the run from the Dog Catcher. I was being thoughtless. Will you all accept my sincerest apologies?" he pleaded, flashing his best showbiz smile.

They all nodded in agreement.

"So what's this mead all about? Is it bubbly?" asked Cheryl, changing the subject swiftly. She took a big sniff of the terracotta pot that Snif and Timmy had brought.

"Mmmm, is that honey I can smell? And if I'm not mistaken, there's a hint of peppermint too," said Cheryl knowingly.

"That is indeed correct: honey, peppermint and the freshest milk from the Big Folk farm. But we are still waiting for the essential ingredient," teased Snif.

"What's that then?" asked Pickle

disparagingly. "One of Cheryl's bottom
burps and a streak of Timmy's snot?"

"Very funny!" said Snif. "For your
information, Timmy's nose doesn't run
anymore, and Cheryl's sorted out her
windypops."

"But what *is* the missing ingredient?"
begged Hamish, licking his lips excitedly.

"Go on! Just tell us Snif," said Top Dog.

"Our pal Lennie is on his way with it. You'll find out soon enough," he replied.

"Oh pleeeeeaaaaaaaaaaasssee," they chorused.

"Okay," sighed Snif. "If you must know, the essential ingredient is Stinkiberry."

"See?" said Pickle triumphantly. "I told you it was going to be horrible."

"It's from the legendary Stinkiberry tree of the Herralayan Mountains in deepest Gibbertibby," continued Snif, ignoring Pickle. "But that's not all. Once we have the Stinkiberry, Badger has to add his famous sparkle and fizz spell. And then ..." he nodded to Cheryl, "... we'll have bubbles too!"

"Good luck with that then, Snif," jeered Pickle. "In case you haven't noticed, Badger's magical neckerchief, the mascot of his spells, is currently missing."

"What? 'Chief's missing? Surely not! We'll all be lost without the neckerchief," cried Snif, peering at Badger through the fog.

Just then, Otto flew in amongst them, and tossed his tassle around haughtily. "Er, I think you'll find that *I'm* more than capable of helping Badger in his hour of need."

Badger shuddered and headed up the lane to see how preparations were going. The others continued catching up with each other.

"So, how does it feel to be a do-gooding member of the community now then, Snif?" sneered Pickle.

"It feels *really* good, Pickle. After all those years I spent on the streets, at least I know how it feels when we get a new stray in."

"Don't you miss all the action and adventure we used to have?"

"Action and adventure? You must be kidding. All I remember is being on the run all the time, and scraping around for food," Snif replied.

"You're getting soft in your old age. Nothing's the same anymore."

"Yes, I heard Pogo Paws went off to pastures new. You must miss him."

"Him? He was even softer than you. I'm glad to be shot of him really. At least now I'm head of the gang."

"Of course you are, Pickle: a gang of one. Well, enjoy it while it lasts," chuckled Snif.

Pickle looked at Snif grumpily and sidled off towards the Crunchy Munchy Chewy Chops.

"What's that noise?" shrieked Cheryl.

"It sounds like quacking to me, and it's getting closer," said Timmy. Out in the lane, Badger could hear the approaching *quacks* too.

Through the eerie mist, seven ducks appeared. They were not walking, nor were they flying ... they were simply *floating*.

"Uh oh!" said Badger looking down at his paws which were soaked through. "It looks like the lane is flooding."

Chapter Four

The birds struggled through the pea-souper to tell Badger what had happened.

Otto gulped and made a hasty retreat from Badger's head, flying off to hide in the fog. Badger groaned as he discovered that when Otto had gone to get water for his unjamming spell, he'd left the hosepipe running. As a result, water was seeping far and wide ... mostly into their lane.

Can things really get any worse, on this, the most exciting night of the year? he thought miserably, running to shut off the hosepipe.

Meanwhile, Cheryl and Dodgy Dave were splashing up and down the lane, twirling umbrellas and doing their "Singing in the Rain" routine. Snif and Timmy were lugging their precious cargo of mead to higher ground. Hamish's ears were sodden, and

Top Dog had tied them on top of his head to stop them getting any wetter.

Otto had returned and was trying in vain to scoop the water away from the lane, one tiny hatful at a time, while the alley cats had taken refuge up the old oak tree.

Badger tried and tried to twist the tap of the hosepipe, but it wouldn't budge. It was completely stuck. Without 'Chief, Otto or anyone else to help him, he closed his eyes and hoped for the best, as he summoned his old faithful anticlockwise spell:

> *"With backwards leap and small rotate,*
> *Take this tap and lubricate."*

He tentatively nudged the tap, and it moved a tiny smidgen. He kept turning ... a little bit more and a little bit more. Soon, the water flow had completely stopped.

He sprinted back to the lane with a bounce in his step. At last, he had managed a successful spell. All — By — Himself!

"Thank goodness, you're back, Badger. We need one of your spells to sort this!" shouted Snif.

Badger looked with renewed confidence at where his neckerchief used to be, and over at Otto. He still crossed his paws for luck.

"Okay, the good news is that the water has stopped, so let's try my *Sneaky Leaky* spell to get rid of all this flooding. Stand back everyone. If this goes wrong, we could all be at a pool party tonight."

Badger stood very still and closed his eyes. Sparkles of light appeared around him as he uttered the words:

"Puddle guddle, splishy sploshy.
Gush and gurgle, wishy washy.
Paws are wet, and water seeps.
Save us from the flooding deeps."
Everyone held their breath.

Then ever so slowly, the waters began to retreat.

Badger breathed a sigh of relief. Another problem sorted.

As the others gathered brushes to sweep away the remaining water from the lane, Badger spotted a single light shining through the still thick fog, further down the lane.

As the light drew closer, Badger saw it was his old pals Lennie and his brother Louie. The light was coming from a bicycle lamp strapped to Lennie's head. He hurried towards them.

"I love your lamp, Lennie. That's ingenious," said Badger. "Thank you both so much for making it on such a dreadful night. I'm sure this weather is nothing like you've seen on your travels."

"We've been globe-trotting for a long time, Badger, so we've learned how to survive in all sorts of conditions" said Lennie solemnly, tapping his bicycle lamp. "And I wouldn't have missed this reunion for the world."

"What's that?" asked Badger pointing at a small wooden box around Lennie's neck.

"*That* is the all-important ingredient for Snif's magical mead."

"We're almost ready to get this party started then," grinned Badger. "Come and see the others."

"Lennie!" shouted Top Dog, Dodgy Dave, Snif and Pickle in unison, as he and his brother emerged from the fog.

"I've got the Stinkiberry, Snif, and I've also brought a photo album of our travels to show you," said Lennie proudly, looking at Louie.

Snif went off to mix his mead, while the others sat down to look at Lennie's pictures, aided by the lamp on top of his head.

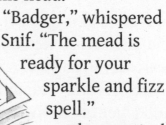

"Badger," whispered Snif. "The mead is ready for your sparkle and fizz spell."

The mystical mutt jumped up and headed for the

earthenware cask. He closed his eyes,
crossed his paws across the pot and said:

Take just three anti-swizzle sticks,
Add fourteen dizzy tizzies,
Stir in a dash of bubble flicks,
And mead is full of fizzes."

The mixture exploded and a hundred
dancing lights burst out with an
effervescent glitz.

"Well, I think that worked after all!"
beamed Badger.

"Erm, not exactly," said Snif, as three
zillion jiggling chicken pox joined their
party. Seeping spots of itchy pus spilled into
the lane as Otto sniggered.

"*What* have you done now?" yelled
Badger crossly at the fez.

"I just thought it would liven things up
a bit with scratchy stings and scabs. It'll
definitely keep us all moving," grinned Otto.

"*This* is meant to be a party, not a sick
bed. All I wished for was for everything to
go to plan, and you have ruined it!" Badger
barked.

The itchy spots were swarming around Cheryl and Dodgy Dave like bees.

"I command you, Otto, to stop this now!" shrieked Badger. "They are about to go on tour again. They can't get the chicken pox. They won't be able to dance."

"I can, and I will, but only if you promise never to put me in the plant pot again, even when 'Chief comes back. I need to fly every day," said Otto.

"You're blackmailing me?" asked Badger with his eyebrows raised to the sky. "Okay, I promise. We'll find a way to let you fly ... always."

At once, Otto flew amidst the spots and scabs, and air-marched them away from the party, across the fog and out of the lane.

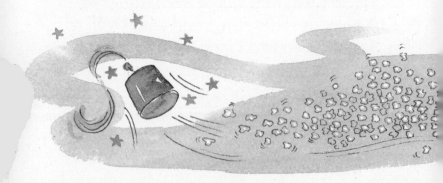

"You've not lost your edge, with or without 'Chief," grinned Snif in admiration.

Badger shrugged, knowing it was really down to Otto that the pox had disappeared.

Meanwhile, Pickle was upsetting the party's latest arrival.

"Lennie, I can't believe you just upped and left us in the lane. How could you manage on your own, without us?" she scoffed.

Lennie, who had been full of good cheer when he arrived, whimpered helplessly.

Louie stepped in. "He wasn't on his o he had me! So, if you've got nothing ni o say then I'd advise you to be quiet."

"This gang reunion, if I can call it that, isn't worth a jot. We're not the gang we used to be. You've all gone namby-pamby. I blame Badger. If he hadn't got involved with us, then we would still be as we always were," replied Pickle huffily.

"Badger? You're blaming Badger? If it hadn't been for him, I'd be behind bars with the Dog Catcher right now ... or worse," said Top Dog.

"Me too," added Dodgy Dave.

"And me," agreed Lennie.

"All you ever talk about is how fabulous Badger is. Doesn't anyone think about how amazing *I've* been, holding everything together in the name of the gang, while you've all been off doing your own things?" screamed Pickle.

"There's nothing amazing about what *you've* done, Pickle!" said Louie angrily.

"And if you're going to blame Badger, then you've no right to be at this party," said Top Dog.

"I'm not fussed about this Goody Two-Shoes party anyway," said Pickle.

"Fine! Well, leave then. No one really wants you here if you're going to be so horrible," said Lennie.

"Leave? You seriously want me to go?" asked Pickle incredulously "In this fog?"

"You said yourself that you don't want to be here, so just go and let the rest of us get on with having a good time," said Top Dog.

"Fine!" snarled Pickle.

"Fine!" shouted the others in reply.

Very slowly, Pickle walked to the end of the lane. No one shouted her to return. Without a backwards glance, she crept under a nearby bush.

After testing a few glasses of mead, Badger and Snif emerged to join the others.

"Where's Pickle?" asked Snif.

"In this fog, it's amazing we can see *anyone*," said Badger.

"She's gone," said the others.

"Gone? What do you mean? I organised this party to cheer her up. How can she have left?" said Badger.

"She was being horrible about us and about you Badger, so we asked her to leave."

Oh no! thought Badger, putting his head in his paws. *Could this night get any worse?*

Otto flew to his side and chuckled. "Your wish is my command, Badger."

Chapter Five

The Earl of Doodlepoppington was back. He strode purposefully down the lane carrying his gifts for the party, excited to see his cousin Badger, who had reunited him with his mother in Persia many moons ago.

As he drew nearer to the party, he heard muffled whimpering. He sniffed around him, and peered through the fog, until he saw a bundle under a bush. He peeked closer. There was Pickle, huddled, damp and very distressed.

"Hello, Pickle," said the Earl cheerfully. "What are you doing out here? Why aren't you with the others at the party?"

"Ugh!" said Pickle crossly. "You're *all* I need tonight. The last time I saw you, you tried to double-cross me."

"My dear girl, that was before I saw the

error of my ways. And you all helped me do that. Now what seems to be the problem here?"

"Problem? You're my only problem right now. I just want to be alone. The others have decided that I'm not fit to attend their stupid party. So leave me to sulk, please."

"What have you done to annoy them this time?" sighed the Earl.

"Nothing! All I did was point out how we used to rumble along together as a gang, causing mayhem along this lane. They've all changed. They're all a bit ... *good* now. Where's the fun in that?"

"And what about Pogo Paws? Does he think this too?" asked the Earl kindly.

"Hah! Pogo Paws left long ago. He ran off to the circus. So it's just me in charge of the gang," snorted Pickle.

"So, you're all on your own now? I can understand you feel angry, but it doesn't have to be like this."

"Oh, so now you're not only an earl, but you're also lord and master of what's good for me?" frowned Pickle.

"Friends are friends, my dear girl, regardless of their flaws. You've got a good bunch there with the gang. If they have changed for the better, they can still be your pals. It's nice to be nice, and it might improve your mood a little."

Pickle turned her back on the Earl and curled up under the bush.

The Earl said: "I'll leave you to it then, because everybody's waiting for me to arrive." He shook his head and swept off down the lane to join the others at the party.

At the party, the alley cats were in full swing. The Meowzik Maker was pumping up the volume and Cheryl and Dodgy Dave were getting down to the beat.

Badger was still glum, even though he was surrounded by several slices of toast.

A figure emerged from the fog. Badger jumped up and threw his paws around the Earl.

"Doodles, am I glad to see you!" grinned Badger.

"Yes, I just met your old pal Pickle in the lane. She seems a bit down in the dumps."

Badger frowned "I know. This party is supposed to be for *her,* and now she's not even here."

"I say, old chap, where's that red raggy thing you've usually got tied around your neck?"

"It's a long story," groaned Badger.

"Never mind! I come bearing gifts: party hats to be exact," said the Earl, thrusting a bulging bag forward.

Everyone clamoured round Badger to look in the bag, which was packed with bright red hats bearing tickly tassles ... just like Otto.

"But I'm the only fez in this lane!" cried an outraged Otto.

The others looked at each other and fell about laughing. The Earl gave out the hats to each party member. Soon, no one knew which of the hats was Otto.

Then one of the hats caught Lennie's eye. "That one must be Otto!" he shrieked "Look! It's moving all on its own." They peered at the fez gliding along the ground.

Two tiny feet emerged from underneath the hat, and they realised it was Cheryl, swamped by the fez.

"It's too big," she giggled. "I can't see where I'm going."

"None of us can in this fog," said Dodgy Dave.

All of a sudden, the fezzes rose up into the air and flew in formation. They all looked upwards in wonder, as the hats performed a double-diamond roll, followed swiftly by a quarter-clover manoeuvre, and

then a whirl of loops and swoops, before each
fez glided perfectly onto their heads.

The hat
on top of Lennie's
head began to rumble.
He looked upwards to see a
shower of confetti cascade down
from his hat.

"I think this one's Otto, because
he's showing off," said Lennie.

Once Lennie was completely covered
from head to paw in the multi-coloured
confetti, Otto whizzed off to tickle everyone
with his tassle. Lennie looked at Otto
flying around in complete admiration. Otto
noticed that Lennie was impressed with his
antics, and puffed out his tassle proudly.
At last, thought the little fez, *someone*

appreciates me!

"Okay," said the Earl taking command. Everything looks good, and smells good. Let's get this party started, right now!"

"Woohoo!" they chorused as they all bounced to the beats. Badger looked on thoughtfully. He was pleased to see his pals enjoying themselves, but he couldn't forget that there were missing guests. 'Chief had vanished, Pickle had been excluded and Pogo Paws was in a circus, far far away.

He needed some help, and he needed it fast, before the reunion could be truly complete.

Chapter Six

The sounds of the party grew fainter, as Badger soared higher and higher through the fog in his beloved Wim-Wim, heading off to visit the only one who could help him see clearly.

Back at the party, Top Dog, Hamish, Dodgy Dave, Cheryl, Snif, Timmy, Lennie, Louie, Otto and the Earl of Doodlepoppington had started a conga line leading up the lane. They were all in high spirits. The midnight hour was not far away.

As Badger landed the Wim-Wim gently in the enchanted forest, he was met by his plucky friend, Baby Unicorn.

"It's unusual to see you on your own Badger. What's up?" asked the unicorn.

Badger sighed.

"Everything has gone wrong. 'Chief has left me and I don't feel as badgical magical anymore. Plus, I tried to organise a reunion party with the gang, to cheer Pickle up, because she's missing Pogo Paws badly. But now she's disappeared too."

"Okay, follow me," said Baby Unicorn wisely. "I'm sure we can get this sorted out."

They made their way along the golden-leaved path towards the famous crystal cave. The fog was far, far below them.

Inside, they walked quietly through avenues of gleaming, shimmering crystals, till they arrived at an archway of glittering stalactites. Badger's eyes widened as they stepped into a chamber of pure purple light.

"Epic!" said Badger, as they stood before a wall of dazzling amethyst crystal. Baby Unicorn nodded to Badger to stay completely still.

"This," said the unicorn, "is the Whispering Wall; the place where you will always hear the truth. Only those who stand in this spot can hear the words of wisdom that are meant for them. Whatever your question, your deepest desire for knowledge will be answered here.

"So, over to you, Badger. Close your eyes and think hard about what it is you really want to know." Badger closed his eyes tightly. He asked where his neckerchief had gone, how he could reunite Pickle properly with her old friends, and how he could get rid of the nuisance that was Otto.

The crystals began to vibrate and pulsate with light. At first he heard mixed murmuring and mumbling, then a fully fledged whisper said: *"Chief has not deserted you, and Pickle's friends are true. When you least expect it, you will have a rendezvous."*

Badger scratched his head, looked at Baby Unicorn and tapped the wall.

"What does that mean then? Is it a riddle?"

"Don't touch the wall, Badger. You must not disrespect the wisdom of the amethyst. Everything you need to know is in your heart," said Baby Unicorn.

"Oops! Sorry, Whispering Wall," bowed Badger politely, still looking a little bewildered.

"Chin up, my friend. It's time for you to rejoin your party. You can't be a party pooper-scooper," winked the unicorn. "And I have my own contribution to make to the festivities."

Baby Unicorn pointed his horn at a box to the side of the Whispering Wall, which was giggling and jiggling. Badger looked at it suspiciously.

"Should I be worried? Will it travel back okay in the Wim-Wim?"

"Of course, Badger. It's only some party poppers and streamers, but they do get excited about being outside of their box."

Badger grabbed the package, said "thank you" to his friend, and boarded the Wim-Wim to head back to the party.

With the Wim-Wim's fog lights on full beam, he came into land at the far end of the lane, feeling much calmer about his missing neckerchief. He had to simply trust that 'Chief would return.

At the party, Cheryl had brought out her karaoke machine and Dodgy Dave was belting out his best rendition of "You ain't nothing but a Hound Dog". The others were jitter-bugging, twisting the night away, and having a happy hootenanny.

Badger stepped out of the Wim-Wim with his box of goodies. In the distance, he heard a muffled jingle-jangle sound. As the clink and clankle drew nearer and louder, he spotted an all too familiar sight.

A pair of big black boots thundered towards him.

The Dog Catcher had returned!

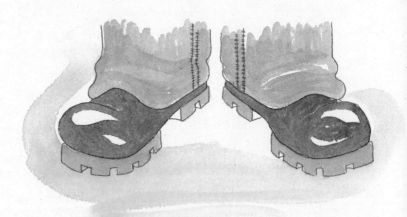

Chapter Seven

Badger gasped and slunk into the murky shadows. Once the Dog Catcher had gone past, he crept out and made his way back to the garden.

The party was in full swing, and the mead was proving very popular.

Little did they all know that Otto had secretly added a few playful ingredients to the mead mix: a sprinkling of agar-agar powder; a handful of flax seeds; and a razz of rhubarb.

"Badger, where have you been? You're missing all the fun," hiccupped Lennie "You have to try some more of the home-made mead. It's amazing!"

"Thanks Lennie, but I need to concentrate on who I've just seen out there in the lane," said Badger darkly.

Snif stopped jiving and tilted his head, "What's that, Badger? Who did you see?"

"Yet another old friend of ours! But one who wasn't invited. I'm afraid the Dog Catcher is back and on the prowl."

The lane went quiet. The music stopped, and everyone huddled around the Mystical Mutt firing questions at him. There was panic afoot.

Suddenly, the Earl stepped into the middle and shouted: "Halt! Keep calm everyone!"

There was a collective hush.

"Now, listen here. What do any of you have to fear from the Dog Catcher? I believe that you're all in good homes or good jobs. Surely you are now all official?"

"That's true," said Top Dog. "Hamish's Big Folk made sure I was micro-chipped when they took me in."

"And I've got a collar now, and needed documents to be able to go on tour," added Dodgy Dave.

"We had to get permits and go through all the correct channels to be able to set up PLOPP, so that must mean we're safe too," said Snif.

"I made sure Lennie had his passport before we could go travelling. Besides which, I'm his guardian now," said Louie proudly. Lennie beamed.

"And of course dear fellows, there's never been any question about my lineage," added the Earl, with just a glimpse of his old pomposity.

They all breathed a sigh of relief and got ready to boogie again.

"Hang on a minute," said Badger, "I think there's someone we've forgotten; someone who is still a stray, with no home. And someone, who is this very minute, in danger, out there in the fog, on her own."

They all turned round and shouted at once "Pickle!"

"So how can we help her then, gang?" asked Badger.

"Why should *we* do anything?" frowned Dodgy Dave "She's been horrible to all of us."

The others muttered and nodded their agreement. Badger stood quietly and listened.

"So tell me, why do you think Pickle was behaving so badly?" asked Badger.

"Because she's always been mean?" offered Snif.

"Maybe she never did, and still doesn't,

like us?" suggested Top Dog.

"Perhaps she's missing Pogo Paws?" said Lennie.

"I think that's it in a nutshell, Lennie," agreed Badger "She sees all of you doing well, being happy, and none of you are on your own. Rather than admit that, I think Pickle was lashing out and pretending she doesn't care."

The others mulled over what Badger had just said. It was Top Dog who spoke up first. "Right, what can we do to get her to safety?"

"Well, I know where she *was,* but I don't know if she'll still be there," said the Earl. "She was under a very damp bush further up the lane. Follow me."

As they all trooped off to find their friend, they could hear the distant thud of the Dog Catcher's boots behind them, and the jingle-jangle of his keys.

"We'll have to be quick," said Badger, sniffing the ground to pick up Pickle's trail. The others did the same.

"She's over here!" yelled Snif. They rushed to the bush where Pickle was sitting defiantly with her paws crossed.

"What?" she said. "Can't a girl get any peace from you lot?"

"Pickle, we don't have time for this right now," said Badger urgently. "The Dog Catcher is right behind us, and he's coming for you. We need to get you back to my garden and hide you in the shed."

"Leave it to me," said Otto the fez, diving off Badger's head and into a spin. Within seconds, the fez had transformed into a red-velvet, rectangular box.

"Wow!" said Badger impressed, "I forgot about your shape-shifting talents."

"You should make use of me more often then," said a voice from one of the cushion tassles.

"Right, Pickle, get in!" ordered Badger.

"I'm not getting in there!" said Pickle

The others lunged forward, grabbed her by the ruff and bungled her in.

"Lennie, sit on the top, and make sure she stays quiet."

They hoisted the box on top of their shoulders and headed towards Badger's garden.

But as they set off down the lane, they bumped slap bang into two big boots.

"So what's going on here then?" glowered the Dog Catcher.

Chapter Eight

"We've run out of chairs for our party," blustered Dodgy Dave, trying to explain the large box, and pointing at his collar.

"We found this in the skip," added Badger.

"I've got a passport now," said Lennie proudly.

"Come and join us later if you want," braved Top Dog, hoping the big boots could still spot his micro-chip tag in the fog.

"Be on your way then, and I might drop in after I've finished my patrol," said the Dog Catcher.

They sighed in relief as the boots trundled on down the lane.

A persistent knocking started up from inside the box.

"Ignore her," said Top Dog. "We have to get her back to the party as quickly as possible."

They reached Badger's garden and released Pickle. The box juddered and exploded into a million sparkles. Soon Otto the Fez was back on top of Badger's head and the box had vanished.

"Awesome!" said Hamish in utter disbelief.

"Right, thank you, Otto. Pickle, get yourself into my shed, please, and stay there until I tell you that the coast is clear. There's toast and warm blankets and you can watch from the window," ordered Badger.

For once, Pickle did exactly as she was told.

The others spread themselves between the garden and the lane and continued to party. The alley cats pumped up the volume as the midnight hour drew closer.

A few minutes later, they heard footsteps clomping towards them. It was the Dog Catcher, and he was smiling.

"So, have I come to the right place? Is this the party? I've brought you all some tasty *slaverpalavers* and *slobberstix* as treats."

"Come this way," drooled Dodgy Dave. They welcomed their old enemy into the party and he looked around for a chair.

"Where's the big box?" asked the Dog Catcher a little puzzled.

"Oh," said Badger, thinking quickly on his paws, "my Big Folk needed it, They're having a party indoors too."

The Dog Catcher knelt on the grass and ruffled their heads.

"I know we've not always seen eye to eye, but I'm only trying to do what's best for dogs without homes."

"But you've got a big scary net," said Lennie.

"And huge boots," added Snif.

"That's only because you can run so much faster than me," smiled the Dog Catcher. "Whenever I catch a dog, I take it to the Dog Home, where there's food, a nice clean bed, fresh water, and company."

"But we heard that when dogs go there, they never come back," whispered Top Dog.

"But you came back, Top Dog, and look at you now with Big Folk to look after you."

"Yes, but to be truthful, I escaped ... as did my friend here, Dodgy Dave."

"I know," sighed the Dog Catcher. "You both gave me a fright when you disappeared. Usually though, dogs aren't quite as cunning as you two, and we find them all homes with Big Folk who can't wait to look after them, and give them lots of love."

Suddenly the shed door burst open.

Pickle stood in one of Dodgy Dave's spotlights with her paws raised above her head.

"That all sounds good to me. Take me in now, Dog Catcher. I'm giving myself up."

The Dog Catcher spun round in surprise.

"Pickle?" he said, "I thought you'd left the lane ages ago to go with Pogo Paws?"

"No, I'm afraid I chose to stay here, but now I'm ready to go to the Dog Home please," she said, pushing her neck forward ready for the Dog Catcher's collar and chain.

Lennie stood up. "But she's not a stray," he said. "She's with us."

Dodgy Dave joined him. "Actually, she's on tour with us."

Snif then rose to his feet, and added "She's got a part-time job at PLOPP, so she can't come, because we need to train her up."

Top Dog stepped forward and said "Our Big Folk took Pickle in this very night, so she's got a home."

Pickle's eyes glistened. She could not believe how her old gang were sticking up for her.

Badger looked from the Dog Catcher to Pickle, and back to the Dog Catcher.

"I think you can definitely strike Pickle

off your 'most wanted' list. Is that correct, Pickle?"

Pickle nodded, unable to speak.

"Well that settles that then. Have a good night, you lot. I must be on my way before the bells chime in the New Year," said the Dog Catcher.

Pickle waited until he was well out of earshot, before hugging each of her old friends in turn.

"I can't believe, after everything I've said and done, that you'd still all defend me like that," she said, trying not to cry.

"That's what friends are for," said Badger wisely.

"Have some of this magical mead, Pickle. We know you still miss Pogo Paws," offered Lennie. Pretty soon, Pickle was enjoying herself and dancing gleefully with the others.

Otto smirked. His added ingredients to the mead were starting to take effect, but none of the revellers had noticed yet.

Over by the shed, Badger picked up the
scent of a freshly delivered p-mail.

It was from Pogo Paws, and it simply said:
"I'm on my way".

Chapter Nine

The fog was thinning as Old Year's Night carried on. The party and its guests were grooving. The food was nearly finished, but the alley cats still had plenty of *oomph* in their Meowzik Maker. The evening was still young.

"What's happened to your fur, Badger?" shrieked Cheryl, "It's all spiky."

Badger pointed at Cheryl "What's happened to yours? You look like a topsy-turvy thistle."

Cheryl gasped, and tried to pat down her fur, but every time she patted, another tuft sprang up.

"And you look like a creeping juniper bush," laughed Badger, spotting Dodgy Dave.

One by one, they saw that the fur of all of their coats was standing on end.

"It's difficult to see in the dark, but if I'm not mistaken, my gorgeous coat has gone a deep shade of purple too," said the Earl disdainfully.

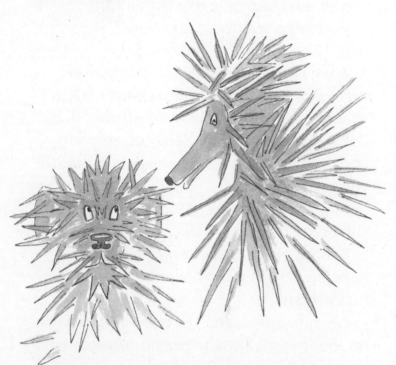

Badger scratched his chin and said, "Right, this has got to be the mead. Lennie, what exactly has the famous stinkiberry done to us all?"

Lennie looked at his brother Louie in panic.

"Badger," said Louie calmly, "I can assure you, we've had this mead many times, and all it's ever done is tasted good. I've never seen it affect anyone like this before."

Otto, who was flying overhead, shook with laughter.

They looked upwards.

"Is this something to do with you, Otto?" shouted Badger sternly.

"I *might* have added a few extra ingredients to the mix," snorted the fez, still tittering. "This *is* supposed to be a party after all. Don't worry, the colour will eventually fade and the spikiness will gradually flop."

"Eventually?" howled Cheryl "We're due back on tour tomorrow!"

"Oops!" said Otto mischievously.

95

"Right, you've had your fun, Otto, and we all think you're *hilarious*. You're always moaning about being excluded, so come down here and have some mead with us too."

"No chance! I'm meant to be red and my tassle is perfectly sleek, thank you very much," shouted the fez, zooming higher still.

Lennie looked longingly after the hat and said: "I wish that fez was mine."

"Really?" said a baffled Badger. "You're welcome to him then, if 'Chief ever returns. In the meantime, I'm ignoring him. See how he likes that!"

The others agreed that to simply ignore the fez seemed like a very good plan indeed.

"Let's get back into the party spirit. So what if we're purple and spiky?" said Hamish cheerfully.

" Yes, show us some magic tricks, Badger," suggested Louie.

Timmy threw him a banana and asked, "Can you straighten that?"

Badger sighed heavily, looked to where his neckerchief had once sat and then raised his eyebrows wearily to Otto the Fez, still giggling above.

"Well, I can try. If I can remember my banana-straightening spell, that is.

"Manyana banana, so ripe and so yellow,
Do me a favour and be a nice fellow.
Why are you curved? Is that your fate?
Just take your bend and now make it straight."

Badger stood back and watched the banana tie itself into a knot. He scratched his chin as the others all fell about laughing. Otto sulked, as no one was laughing at him anymore. In fact, it was as if he wasn't even there.

"Well, it's not quite a straight banana, Badger, but I think it's funnier like that. Any more tricks?" guffawed Dodgy Dave.

"Enough!" giggled Badger. "Now, why don't you all tell me your plans for the year ahead. Has anyone got any New Year's resolutions?"

"Yes," piped up Top Dog. "Hamish and I are going to volunteer to help at PLOPP once a week with Snif and Timmy."

"That's very admirable, Top Dog. Anyone else?" asked Badger.

"Yes, Cheryl's got a plan," said Dodgy Dave nudging his dancing partner. Cheryl's eyes widened as she took centre stage and explained. "We're starting free dancing classes after this next tour for our footloose four-legged friends."

"Wow!" said Badger nodding appreciatively. "I know there will be lots of eager pals who will be delighted to follow in your footsteps."

"And we've got a recipe book coming out with all the dishes we've created at PLOPP," said Timmy. "It's called *Classic Creations from PLOPP on the Lane* and the famous chef, Delilah Whiff, has written the introduction. It's really exciting. We're hoping Miss Whiff will be able to join us for the launch."

"Snif, Miss Whiff and Timmy! What a dream team that will be down at PLOPP! Well done, you two. You've both worked so hard," said Badger proudly.

"Our next trip is to an ashram in Bangalore, to chill out," said Lennie looking at his brother Louie happily.

"Aha!" said Badger "So the Zen Den in our last adventure made a bit of an impact?"

Lennie blushed.

The Earl of Doodlepoppington was next to reveal his plans. "Well, my dear boy, I'm thinking of expanding my Pooch Parlour empire to include other planets in our solar system. After all, I've already conquered the world."

"Okay," said Badger mystified. "And you know for sure, there's a market there?"

"There certainly is on Planet Sirius, so that's where I'll start," said the Earl smugly.

"And what about you Pickle?" asked Badger gently.

Pickle stood up, amidst her friends and admitted, "I wish I could start my New Year with Pogo Paws. I should have gone with him to the circus when I had the chance."

The others patted her kindly. Otto, who was now trying to get in everyone's good books, flew around her and tickled her on her tummy with his tassle to make her laugh. Badger smiled, nodded knowingly and said: "Well, if at first you don't succeed, Pickle, try again."

Pickle stared at him, baffled.

Finally, Badger beckoned the fez. "How about you, Otto? Do you have plans for the New Year?"

"I do, I do," said Otto meekly.

"Well, please share them with us all. This should be interesting," said Badger.

"I vow to be more obedient, less cheeky, but most importantly, I'm going to start up my own squadron of red fezzes: an aerobic flying-formation skylark. I, of course, will be flight leader," announced Otto, tilting upwards and twirling like a gyroscope in the air.

"Wow!" said Badger. "Well, we'll all be expecting a spectacular fly-past when 'Chief returns.

Otto smiled and waved his tassle.

As they had been chatting, they hadn't noticed that the fog had cleared completely. The midnight sky was ablaze with stars.

Badger looked up and saw a familiar lone cloud hovering high above.

It was Nippy Nimbus, his grumpy cloud crony.

Chapter Ten

"Happy New Year, Nippy!" shouted Badger up into the sky.

"It's still Old Year's Night. There's still a minute left. It's bad luck to wish me Happy New Year before it's actually Happy New Year" grumbled Nippy Nimbus.

"Well, Happy Old Year then," chuckled the Mystical Mutt.

"Why are you purple? I haven't had any purple rain recently. And I think you've overdone it with the fur gel. You are totally spiky," cackled the cloud.

"On a special night like this, we need to ... erm... look our best," Badger blustered.

"Well, if that's your best, I dread to see your worst," sneered Nippy.

"Quick, everyone," said Badger. "It's nearly New Year."

The rest of the party gathered together in a circle and looked skyward.

Top Dog counted down from sixty.

Hamish joined in at fifty, along with the alley cats.

Cheryl and Dodgy Dave entered the count at forty.

Snif and Timmy chipped in at thirty seconds.

At just twenty seconds to go before the brand new year, Lennie and Louie linked paws with the others.

At ten seconds, the Earl put his arm around Badger and Pickle. They began the final exciting countdown.

"Ten!" they shouted.

"Nine ... eight ... seven ... six ... five ... four ... three ... two ... and one!"

"Happy New Year!" they screamed in delight to one another.

Around them, a cavalcade of fireworks exploded into the sky in a dazzling shower of sparkling colours.

"Happy New Year, Nippy!" yelled Badger "Can't you give me a tiny smile, just for once?"

and the Flying Fez

Nippy Nimbus shuddered and shouted: "I'll make it my New Year's resolution to smile just this once then. Now look, I have a surprise for you!"

As they all watched the feast of starbursts in the sky, balloons floated down from Nippy Nimbus. Badger peered closer. He was sure he had spotted a red and white polka dot parachute amidst the balloons.

Could it be? Badger thought hopefully.
Could this really be 'Chief bringing me New Year cheer?

Cheryl pointed excitedly into the sky.
"Someone's arriving by balloon flight.
Look!"

They looked on in awe as 'Chief landed
softly on the grass, swaddling a bundle.
Badger ran towards his beloved neckerchief.

"At long last, 'Chief, you've come home.
You have no idea how much I've missed
you."

But 'Chief wasn't the only surprise guest
at the party.

The neckerchief unravelled from its
precious cargo to reveal none other than
the gang's missing member, and the long-
lost friend of Pickle.

It was Pogo Paws, live, and in the fur.
Pickle was dumbstruck.

"Happy New Year, Pickle! It's really me,"
said Pogo Paws, a little dizzy from the flight.

The others stood back respectfully,
waiting for Pickle's reaction. Badger tied

'Chief back around his neck, tapped him and whispered "Thank you. But how could you leave without telling me where you were going?"

"For once," explained 'Chief, "Otto was right. You wouldn't have been able to resist telling Pickle that Pogo Paws was coming. It *had* to be a surprise. Sorry, Badger."

"You're back now, and that's all that matters," said Badger gratefully.

Pickle stepped nervously towards Pogo Paws. "Is it really you? Or am I dreaming?"

"It's definitely me, Pickle. Pinch me. I'm real," said Pogo Paws light-heartedly.

Top Dog, Dodgy Dave, Snif, Lennie, Badger and the others all cheered.

"Good to have you back, Pogo Paws. She's been a nightmare without you," said Top Dog.

"Are you staying? You wouldn't leave me again, would you?" asked Pickle.

Pogo Paws looked at Pickle with longing and said: "I never want to leave you again, Pickle." They hugged. The rest of the gang applauded and Badger said: "At last, the old gang is finally all back together again. Happy New Year everyone!"

The remaining drops of mead were passed around, and there was much celebration.

A peeved Otto floated around Badger's head sighing heavily.

"Now that your beloved 'Chief is back, am I going to be consigned to your dusty old plant pot again. Badger?" he asked with a heavy heart.

"Oh Otto, you've given me so many laughs this short while, that I'd hate to put you back in the plant pot, but this mutt ain't big enough for both you and 'Chief. I don't know what to do."

"But you promised that you *wouldn't* put me back in the plant pot if I got rid of the chicken pox," wailed Otto.

Badger scratched his chin. He'd forgotten

about the chicken pox, and a promise was a promise. All of a sudden, 'Chief started to wriggle around Badger's neck and pointed towards Lennie.

"I know!" piped up Lennie. "Can I have Otto? Please? We're stopping off in Turkey en route to Bangalore. Otto, isn't that where you're from?"

Otto nodded enthusiastically.

Badger looked sceptical.

"I'd look after him," said Lennie eagerly. "I'd train him. And I'd let him out to fly every day."

Badger looked at Otto. Otto winked at Badger.

"Okay Lennie, it

sounds like a plan. And good luck with the training."

Otto fixed himself firmly on Lennie's head and tickled his nose with his tassle.

Lennie put on his best commanding voice and said: "Otto, sit!"

Chapter Eleven

It was dawn on the first day of the brand new year. All was quiet, but for a few dull beats still bumping on the Meowzik Maker's turntable. The food was finished and the mead had been drunk dry. A few of the party guests were slumped — half-snoozing, half-purple, half-spiky — around the lane and Badger's garden. The alley cats stretched and yawned.

Louie nudged Lennie gently from his slumber. "Come on, brother. We have a flight to catch."

Lennie woke with a start, scratched his head and spotted Otto the Fez soaring happily above. He remembered his vow to train the pesky hat, and take him with him on his travels, and groaned.

Cheryl already had her curlers in, and

was adding the finishing touches to her lip gloss. She tugged at Dodgy Dave's collar, who was snoring deeply. "Get up, you. We've got a show tonight."

The Earl lay fast asleep with an eye mask and ear plugs.

Top Dog, Snif, Hamish and Timmy started to clear up.

Badger was busy teaching 'Chief his best boomerang spell.

"Boomerangs always come back, 'Chief. So I want us both to know this spell inside out. I'm not risking losing you again," said Badger gently.

"But I wasn't actually *lost*, Badger, and I did come back. I've explained why I couldn't tell you. However, if boomerang spells make you happy, then let's do it," said 'Chief folding itself into a big smiley face.

Pogo Paws and Pickle woke up in the shed together. Pickle rubbed her eyes in disbelief as Pogo Paws turned towards her smiling.

"So you're awake then. It's just like the old days," yawned Pickle, who hadn't slept a wink.

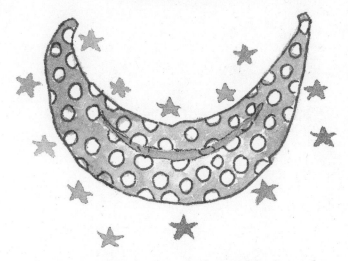

"I've missed you so much, Pickle," said Pogo Paws gently.

"I know," said Pickle. "I've missed you too, my old pal."

As Badger and the others waved goodbye to Lennie, Louie, Cheryl, Dodgy Dave and Otto, the mischievous fez, Pickle started firing questions at Pogo Paws.

"So, how did you get here? I thought the only way you could reach your circus was through a portal in the enchanted forest."

"Correct!" said Pogo Paws.

"But I thought it had to be at a solar eclipse, and last time it involved a minotaur and an enchanting exchange," added Pickle.

"It did ... last time. But this time, 'Chief helped," said Pogo Paws, tapping his nose knowingly.

"So does this mean you can't return?" said Pickle hopefully.

"Not entirely. 'Chief showed me how to get home, but only if I'm not on my own," said Pogo Paws shyly.

"Not on your own? Why, who are you taking with you?" barked Pickle.

"Well, I was very much hoping that would be you," grinned Pogo Paws bashfully.

An incredible rumpus erupted from the shed as Pickle jumped up and down in glee.

Badger, Timmy, Snif, Hamish and Top

Dog all looked at each other in delight. Even the Earl awoke with the excitement in the air.

"Looks like Pogo Paws has given Pickle some good news," said Top Dog.

"Maybe he's back for good," said Hamish hopefully.

"Or perhaps, he's taking her with him," said Snif.

Back in the shed, Pogo Paws was mapping out a plan for Pickle. It involved Badger's Wim-Wim.

"You see," said Pogo Paws, "here's what we have to do. Now let me try to remember what 'Chief said. Yes, that's right: our wish to get back to the circus together must be really strong enough to drive us forward, and then the portal will open. What we think about, we bring about ... or something like that."

"So are you asking me to definitely come with you, Pogo Paws?" asked Pickle.

"I'm definitely asking you to accompany me on the greatest adventure of our lives," said Pogo Paws seriously.

"Then, I'm in. I'm ready. Let's go," said Pickle breathlessly.

They burst out of the shed to a round of applause from the others.

"About time, you two," grinned Badger. "Now, let me get the Wim-Wim ready for departure."

Badger filled the travelling machine with a gallon of haboba juice, and patted it on the side. "Do your best my Wim-Wim for a wowser to wind the weather up on a wet day. You know where you need to go with these two honoured guests."

Pogo Paws and Pickle climbed the ladder and jumped aboard. They waved their cheerios to the others, and waited for lift-off.

Hovering above and waiting patiently was Nippy Nimbus who was still smiling ... sort of.

✦Chapter ✦Twelve✦

The Wim-Wim soared into the sky on a fresh breeze, purring and gurgling its joy at its first assignment of a brand new year. Pogo Paws and Pickle looked down and caught a last fond glimpse of their friends. As the Wim-Wim turned towards the duck pond, they saw Badger, Top Dog, Snif, Hamish and Timmy clearing up after the party.

"So how was Pogo Paws able to get back to here?" asked Hamish. "I mean he was there, then he was here, and now he's going back there!"

"And how is he able to return now with Pickle?" added Top Dog.

"I thought there was a portaloo involved," said Hamish.

"A *portal,* Hamish," giggled Badger. "And you're right. Last time, it required my most powerful magic, plus a little help from Captain Bravebark."

"Captain Bravebark from the Ring of Brodgar?" remembered Timmy, "I've met him, haven't I, Badger?"

"That's right Timmy, a long time ago. What an adventure that was!"

Above them, the Wim-Wim circled once more before shooting off for its destination.

"Goodbye, old oak tree. Goodbye, lane. Goodbye, duck pond," shouted Pickle.

"Goodbye everyone!" added Pogo Paws.

122

Back in Badger's garden, lots of Happy New Year p-mails were arriving. Badger sat down, feeling a little flat. It was always the way after a party, when the guests had nearly all gone.

"Cheer up, Badger," said Top Dog. "Look, there's a confidential p-mail here just for you." Badger plodded over to the fence, where he sniffed the p-mail. It was from Pogo Paws.

"I arrived at your party last night empty-handed. So, I feel it right that I make amends. I've made a reservation at the Delish Deli round the corner. I've booked a booth, so whoever is still around can join you. Please go, enjoy it and have a feast on me."

"Wow!" shouted Badger to the others, licking his lips. "Is anyone else hungry?"

Top Dog, Snif, Hamish, Timmy and the now totally awake Earl all followed Badger to the Delish Deli, and took their places in their very own VIP booth.

As they ordered their various favourite dishes, Badger raised a tumbler to their

absent friends and said: "Should auld acquaintance be forgot."

"Let's drink a cup of kindness here," added the Earl, smiling at them all.

"For Auld Lang Syne," they all sang together.

They feasted on a buffet of Beefy Brutus Wellies, Pure Fishcake Belly Timber and Savoury Shoot Stew.

For a while no one spoke, until Top Dog said:

"The truth is, without you, Badger, and all your mystical ways, we wouldn't all be where we are today."

"Here, here," added Snif. "I'm sure I'd still be in trouble." He looked fondly at Timmy, remembering how the little cat had once rescued him from danger.

"You should award yourself one of your own badges," suggested Timmy, polishing his own shiny Badger Badge.

Badger looked bashful and said: "You did it all by yourselves. I just lent you a helping paw and a bit of magic. Still, it's going to be quiet around here with everyone gone."

"We'll still be here. We're only up the lane at

PLOPP. Pop in anytime, and you must come to the launch of our book," said Snif and Timmy.

"And there's always a few slices of toast on the go at ours," said Hamish and Top Dog.

"Thanks, but I think my work here is done. Maybe it's time for me to go travelling too," said Badger.

When they had finished eating, they said their goodbyes and thanked Badger for a brilliant party. All agreed that Pogo Paws' treat was a truly excellent New Year's Day dinner.

As Hamish, Top Dog, Snif, Timmy and the Earl left the Deli to head homewards, Badger sat back and patted his neckerchief. He looked out at the low winter sun.

"What a badgical-magical job well done. I wonder where this year will take us 'Chief."

He left the Deli and trundled back to his garden. As he did, he heard the familiar clanking and clunking of his trusty Wim-Wim. He looked up and saw it gliding towards him.

Its passengers had gone, and just behind it was the most amazing double rainbow.

"Epic!" smiled Badger, walking over to the sundial, ready to greet the Wim-Wim.

It landed softly beside him. Its ladder folded down and its golden key shone. Badger climbed the steps and took a seat. Inside was a shimmering envelope, in fine silver organza. He held it in his paws and pondered.

He opened it carefully, and discovered a silver invitation card from Captain Bravebark. It read:

> *For today it seems, your work here is done.*
> *Now, it's time to have more fun.*
> *Let the Wim-Wim guide you to pastures new,*
> *Where thrilling adventures await you.*

Badger smiled. He leaned over and turned the golden key. The Wim-Wim rose upwards, and they took off in the midday sky.

In the distance, he spied a V-shaped formation of sixteen flying fezzes. *Otto had kept his word about a fly-past,* he thought, glad that the fez was now free of the plant pot and able to fly forever more.

As he sat back down to enjoy the flight, he thought, *So this year isn't actually going to be so quiet.*

This was his mission after all ... and he chose to accept it.